SPOTTY

WRITTEN BY JENNY BRAHNEY
ILLUSTRATED BY JENNY BRAHNEY

PublishAmerica
Baltimore

First printing

ISBN: 978-1-4560-1360-8
PUBLISHED BY PUBLISHAMERICA, LLLP
www.publishamerica.com
Baltimore

Printed in the United States of America

To Gaby, Christopher and Janice
for boundless love and support

Look at all the pretty flowers!
Can you see a ladybug?
Yes, it's a ladybug Mommy
with her new baby **Spotty**.

1

And here is Daddy with his black hat!
He is so happy and is telling everyone
about his new baby **Spotty**.
He is even ringing the bluebells.

Spotty and his parents live in a mushroom house. Spotty is playing, can you see him?

Uncle Dot is coming to take **Spotty** for a walk.

5

Oh, what lovely music.
Spotty loves the music and wants to be a musician too
"No," says his uncle, "you are a ladybug!"

7

A big pine tree! **Spotty** and his uncle look around. How beautiful it is! Can you see the birds?

Spotty asks if he will grow big wings? "No," says his uncle, "you are a ladybug!"

9

Spotty and uncle Dot stop for a snack.
A bee makes sure that everyone is safe.
The bee has a powerful sting, whispers Uncle Dot.

"Will I have a powerful sting too?", asks **Spotty**
"No," says his uncle, "you are a ladybug!"

11

Spotty wanders off by himself.
Oh no Spotty, you'll get lost!
But what does he see?
A little man dressed in red. Is he sleeping?

13

What did **Spotty** find?
Little men helping all his forest friends.
"Can I paint too?", asks Spotty
"No," says one little man, "you are a ladybug!"

15

"You are too little to be out by yourself.
Grasshopper will take you home,
Come visit when you are all grown!"

Grasshopper runs so fast!
Spotty is glad, this place looks scary!
"Will I be able to run like you?", asks **Spotty**
"No," says grasshopper, "you are a ladybug!"

"This is the bus stop, it will take you home!
Be a good boy now!
Bye!"

21

A flutterbus! Wow! Oh what fun!
"Maybe I'll be a bus too when I am grown."
Spotty was so excited that he fluttered around and ...

landed on a finger!
"Look a ladybug!" says the little girl, "he'll bring us luck!
Spotty is so happy!
"Now I know who I am, a good luck charm!
Mommy, Daddy, I am coming home!"

27